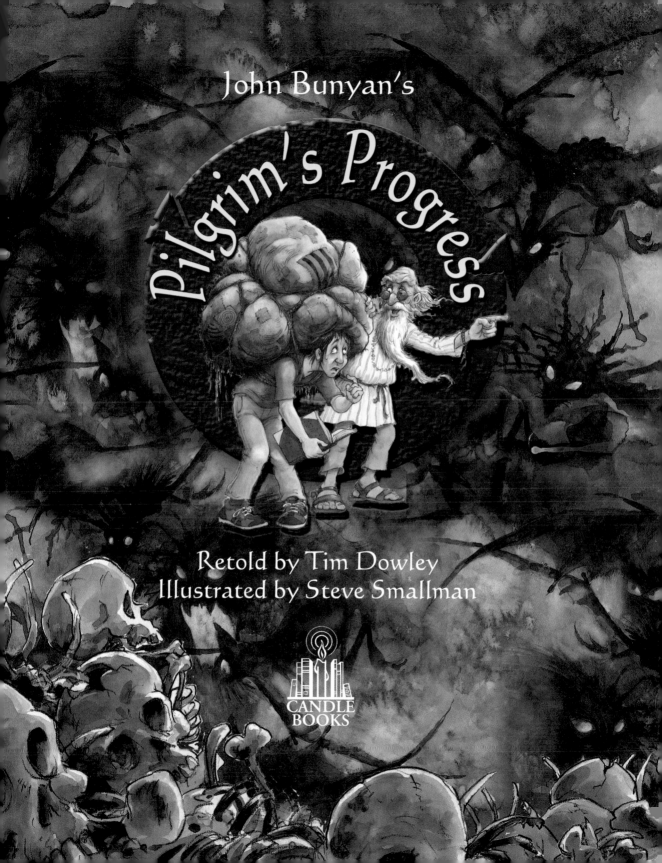

John Bunyan's

Pilgrim's Progress

Retold by Tim Dowley
Illustrated by Steve Smallman

CANDLE
BOOKS

Contents

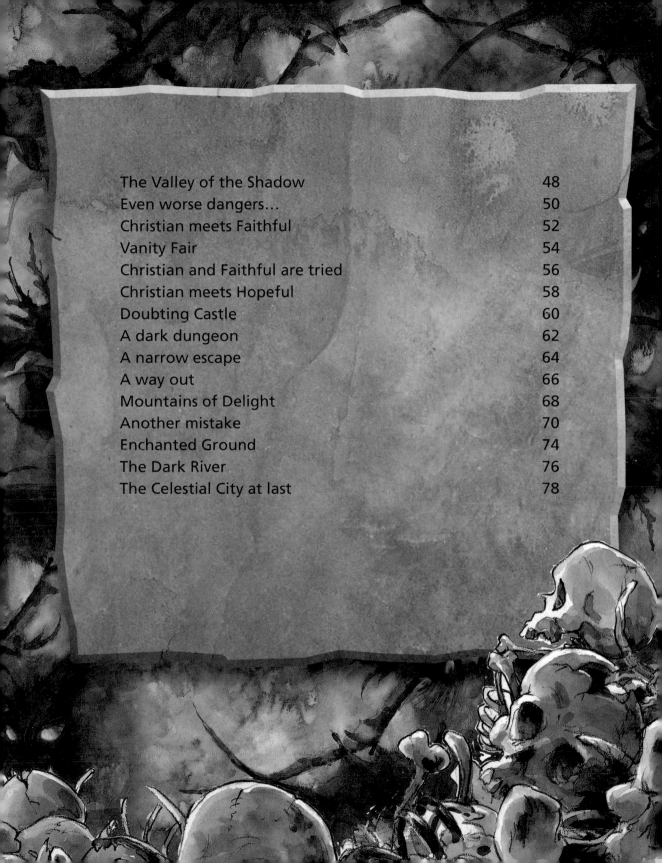

The man in the dream

I DREAMED THAT I SAW a man with a book in his hand and a great burden on his back. I saw him open the book and read it. And as he read, he wept.

Then he cried, "What shall I do to be saved?"

This man lived in the City of Destruction. He had read in his book that the city was going to be burnt with fire from heaven. He would die, and his wife and four sons too, unless they could find a way to escape.

So Christian (that was his name) went home to tell his family. They were very worried – not because they believed what he told them, but because they thought he'd gone quite mad.

It was getting late, and, hoping a good night's sleep might settle him, they put him to bed.

But, instead of sleeping, Christian spent the night moaning and weeping. When morning came, they asked how he felt.

"Worse!" he said. "Even worse!"

6

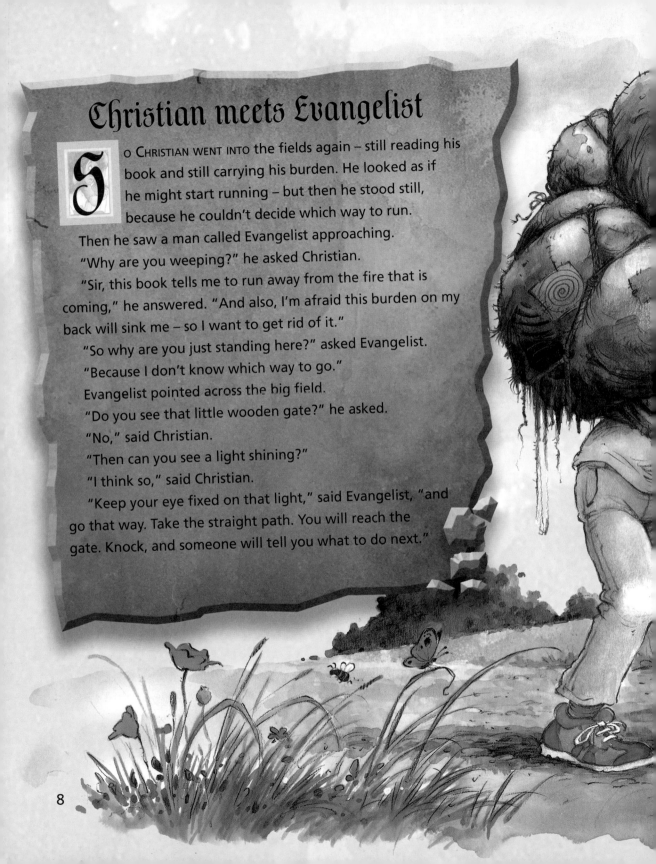

Christian meets Evangelist

SO CHRISTIAN WENT INTO the fields again – still reading his book and still carrying his burden. He looked as if he might start running – but then he stood still, because he couldn't decide which way to run.

Then he saw a man called Evangelist approaching.

"Why are you weeping?" he asked Christian.

"Sir, this book tells me to run away from the fire that is coming," he answered. "And also, I'm afraid this burden on my back will sink me – so I want to get rid of it."

"So why are you just standing here?" asked Evangelist.

"Because I don't know which way to go."

Evangelist pointed across the big field.

"Do you see that little wooden gate?" he asked.

"No," said Christian.

"Then can you see a light shining?"

"I think so," said Christian.

"Keep your eye fixed on that light," said Evangelist, "and go that way. Take the straight path. You will reach the gate. Knock, and someone will tell you what to do next."

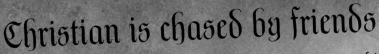

Christian is chased by friends

HRISTIAN'S FRIENDS had come out to watch him. Some of them mocked him and others threatened him. But two men decided to try to fetch him back – one called Obstinate, the other Changeable.

They ran after him and soon caught him up.

"Why have you come?" Christian asked.

"To persuade you to come back with us," they said.

"Then you're wasting your time," said Christian. "Because you live in the City of Destruction. *You* come with *me*."

"What!" said Obstinate " – leave behind our home and friends?"

"Yes! You see, I'm seeking a never-ending kingdom, where we will live for ever. Read about it in my book…"

"Nonsense!" cried Obstinate. "Bother your old book! Come back with us!"

"I won't!"

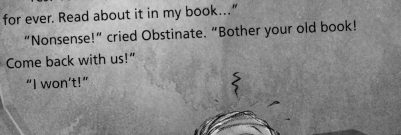

Until now, Changeable had kept quiet; but now he spoke up.

"If what Christian says is true, I'm going with him."

"Do as you please," said Obstinate. "I'm going home. I won't go a step further with two such great idiots."

And so they parted. Obstinate went back, but Christian and Changeable went on, talking ten to the dozen.

"Tell me more, Christian," said Changeable, "about the place we're going to."

"There they will give us crowns of glory, and clothes shining like the sun."

"That sounds great! Anything else?"

"There won't be any more crying," said Christian. "The Owner of the Place will wipe every tear from our eyes."

"I'm glad to hear it. Come on, let's get moving."

"I'm afraid I can't walk any faster," said Christian, "with this burden on my back."

The Slough of Despond

AS CHRISTIAN AND CHANGEABLE hurried on, they came to a bog called the Slough of Despond. And, before they knew what was happening, both of them had fallen in. They wallowed around in the bog, getting muddier and muddier.

Because of the burden on his back, Christian began to sink – first knee-deep, then waist-deep – into the disgusting swamp.

"Christian, where are we?" shouted Changeable.

"I've no idea!" said Christian.

Now Changeable began to get cross.

"Is this the reward you promised? If we've had such bad luck at the very start, what can we expect before the journey ends?"

And Changeable scrambled out of the Slough on the side nearest his house, and ran home for a hot bath.

Meanwhile, Christian was struggling to reach the other side of the bog. When at last he got there, he couldn't haul himself out because of the burden on his back.

Just then, a man called Help came along.

"Whatever are you doing in there?" he asked. "Didn't you see the stepping-stones?"

"I fell in before I saw the danger," said Christian

"Here," said Help, "give me your hand."

And Help pulled him out and got him back on firm ground.

So Christian continued his way towards the little wooden gate.

14

Christian meets Wordly Wiseman

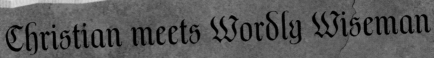

BUT MORE TROUBLE WAS IN STORE. A man called Mr. Worldly Wiseman, who lived nearby in a town called Earthly Ways, was crossing the field.

As soon as they met, he asked Christian, "Hey! Where do you think you're going with such a huge burden?"

"To that little wooden gate."

"Have you no wife and children?" asked Mr. Worldly Wiseman.

"Yes," replied Christian. "But I'm so weighed down, I don't enjoy them any more."

"Who told you to start out on this perilous journey?"

"A man came called Evangelist."

"I thought so!" said Worldly Wiseman. "He's always leading people astray. There's no more difficult road in the world than this one he's sent you on. I can see from your muddy clothes that you've already fallen into the Slough of Despond. But that's only the start! The way you're going, you'll meet far worse – lions, dragons, darkness and death. Don't risk your life listening to a stranger like him.

"Listen to me – after all, I'm much older than you – in that village over there lives a man called Mr. Law. He's an expert at helping people off with their burdens. He's cured any number of people who were being driven crazy by their burdens."

Christian leaves the path

CHRISTIAN WAS MORE THAN READY to listen to Mr. Worldly Wiseman and leave the straight path.

"Which way is this Mr. Law's house?" he asked.

"See that high hill?" asked Mr. Worldly Wiseman, "Go past that, and the first house you'll come to is Mr. Law's."

But Mr. Worldly Wiseman had directed Christian down the wrong road. What he didn't tell him was that the high hill was very frightening. It seemed to hang over the road – so far that Christian was scared it would fall on him. And, even worse, fire flashed from it. Because of his burden, Christian could easily have fallen, and burnt to death. He shook with fear.

18

19

Christian is ashamed

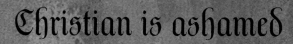

THAT VERY MOMENT, who should appear but Evangelist, with a face so stern that Christian blushed with shame.

"Aren't you the man I found crying outside the City of Destruction?" asked Evangelist.

"Yes, sir."

"Didn't I send you to the little wooden gate?"

"Yes, sir," replied Christian.

"How come you've turned aside so quickly?"

"You see, sir, I met a man who told me I'd find a someone in that village who could take off my burden. He said he'd show me an easier way than the way you sent me."

Then Evangelist said, "You've listened to the advice of Mr. Worldly Wiseman rather than the Word of God. Mr. Law can't free you from your burden – he's just a great cheat."

As he spoke, there was a deafening clap of thunder.

"How stupid I was to listen to Worldly Wiseman," muttered Christian, and turned back quickly.

He didn't feel safe till he was back on the road he had left.

At the wooden gate

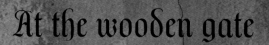

BUT WHEN CHRISTIAN GOT NEARER to the little wooden gate, he saw it was shut. And as he reached it, he heard an arrow fly past his ear. Looking round in fright, he saw on the hill opposite a castle with dark figures on its towers.

Over the little wooden gate it said:

KNOCK, AND IT SHALL OPEN TO YOU.

Christian didn't wait; he knocked with all his might.

A second arrow narrowly missed him.

"Who's there?" called a voice.

"A poor pilgrim with a burden. I'm from the City of Destruction and I'm going to the Celestial City."

To his relief, the gate quickly opened, and a hand pulled him in.

"Who's shooting those arrows?" Christian asked the Gate-keeper, who was called Goodwill.

"That castle belongs to Beelzebub, the Prince of the Devils," said the Gate-keeper. "His soldiers shoot at anyone who tries to enter. They try to kill you before you reach safety."

"Then I'm lucky to be alive," said Christian.

Christian talks to Goodwill

"WHY ARE YOU ON YOUR OWN?" asked Goodwill.

"Because none of my friends saw the danger."

"Didn't anyone follow you?" asked the Gate-keeper.

"Changeable came a little way, till we both fell in the Slough of Despond," Christian answered. "After that he wouldn't come any further."

"Poor man!" said Goodwill. "But isn't it worth a few risks when the Celestial City is your goal?"

"I'm no better," said Christian. "I nearly turned aside too, after listening to Worldly Wiseman. I don't know what would have become of me if Evangelist hadn't met me again. And I'm still terribly uncomfortable with this burden on my back. However hard I try, I can't seem to shift it."

"No human can get it off," said Goodwill. "But keep to the straight and narrow path, and it will lead you to the Place of Freedom."

So Christian prepared to continue his journey.

"How much further is it?" he asked himself, as he plodded on.

At the Explainer's House

AFTER WALKING SOME TIME, Christian came to the Explainer's House, which was big and mysterious. Goodwill had told Christian that the Explainer could pass on some useful tips for his journey.

Christian knocked at the door.

"What can I do for you?" asked the Explainer.

"Sir," said Christian, "I'm going to the Celestial City, and I was told you could show me some things that might help me."

"Then come on in," said the Explainer.

He led Christian into a dark and dismal room, where a man was sitting in an iron cage. He looked very sad.

"Who is this man?" Christian asked.

"Ask him," said the Explainer.

"Who are you?" asked Christian.

"I was once a pilgrim," answered the man. "And I thought I was on my way to the Celestial City."

"But why did you to end up in this cage?"

"I didn't keep watch," said the man. "So now I'm kept in this iron cage. I can't get out."

"Remember what you have seen," the Explainer whispered to Christian.

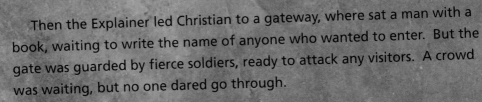

Then the Explainer led Christian to a gateway, where sat a man with a book, waiting to write the name of anyone who wanted to enter. But the gate was guarded by fierce soldiers, ready to attack any visitors. A crowd was waiting, but no one dared go through.

Finally a bold man came up.

"Write down my name, sir," he said to the man with the book.

Then he drew his sword and rushed at the soldiers, who fought him fiercely. But, after a nasty scrap, the man cut his way to safety.

"I think I know the lesson of this man," said Christian.

"My safety depends not on being clever, but on being brave."

And so he continued on his way.

Christian loses his burden

WE DON'T KNOW how Christian's burden first got on his back. But he'd never wanted so badly to get rid of it. So Christian started to run – or did his best to, with that great load on his back.

At the foot of a hill, he passed an open tomb. Above it, he found himself by a cross. As the shadow of the cross fell over him, suddenly the burden dropped from his shoulders and fell right off his back. It tumbled down the hill into the tomb – and he never saw it again. Ever.

Christian just couldn't believe it!

He was astonished that gazing at the cross had set him free.

As he stood there, three Shining Ones appeared.

The first said, "You are washed clean."

The second took away his muddy clothes, and gave him bright new ones.

The third handed him a paper scroll. "Guard this carefully," he said. "Only give it up when you reach the gate of the Celestial City."

Christian felt as light as air. He gave three jumps for joy, and went on, singing:

He who would valiant be
'Gainst all disaster,
Let him in constancy
Follow the Master.
There's no discouragement
Shall make him once relent
His first avowed intent
To be a pilgrim.

Christian meets intruders

THERE WAS A WALL on each side of this stretch of road. As Christian set off again – free of his burden – two strangers suddenly jumped over the wall. One was called Mr. On-the-Surface and the other Mr. Pretender.

"Excuse me!" Christian said. "Where have you come from?"

"We were born in the Land of Emptiness, and we're on our way to the Heavenly City," they replied.

"Then why did you jump over the wall, instead of coming through the little wooden gate? Don't you know that anyone who climbs in a different way is a thief?"

"It's a long way to the wooden gate," answered Mr On-the-Suface. "Our people always take this short-cut. They've done it for hundreds of years, so it can't be wrong."

"But it's against the rules."

"It doesn't matter *how* we got in," said the men. "If we're in, we're in."

"I walk by the Master's rules; you go your own way," said Christian.

The two men didn't answer; they just looked at each other and laughed.

The three continued together, until they reached a cross-roads. One wide road went left; another wide road went right; but the narrow road went straight on – up the great, black Hill Difficulty. Which road would they all choose?

Mr. On-the-Surface chose to go left, which led him into a dark wood. This road was called Danger, and he lost his way for ever.

Mr. Pretender chose to go right, which led him onto rough ground, full of hummocks and holes. This road was called Ruin. He stumbled and fell, and never got up again.

The Hill Difficulty

CHRISTIAN looked at both the other roads, and then started to walk briskly straight up the hill. But soon he was wondering if he'd made a good choice. He went from running to walking; from walking to clambering; and soon it was so steep he was slithering on his hands and knees.

Half-way to the top, just as he was about to give up, he spied a shelter for tired pilgrims, built by the Lord of the Hill. Here Christian sat down gratefully to rest. He pulled out the paper scroll the Shining One had given him and read it to cheer himself up. Soon, he'd fallen fast asleep in the afternoon sunshine.

When he woke, it was evening, so he hurried on. Suddenly, he heard running footsteps coming towards him. Out of the twilight appeared two men – Scared and Distrust.

"Whatever's the matter?" asked Christian. "You're going the wrong way."

"We were going to the Heavenly City, and had climbed the Hill Difficulty," said Scared. "But the further we went, the more dangers we met – so we're giving up and going back."

"We met two lions on the road," added Distrust. "If we'd have come within paws' reach, they'd have torn us to pieces."

So Scared and Distrust ran back down the hill, leaving Christian in a fix. "If I go on, I'll die," he told himself. "And if I go back to my own country, I'll die too. What shall I do?"

Then he remembered his scroll, and felt for it in his coat. But though he looked everywhere for it, he couldn't find it. He must have dropped it! Without it, he could never enter the Celestial City. There was nothing for it but to go back.

"What a fool I've been," he told himself, as he retraced his steps, searching everywhere. It was growing darker all the time, and the night was full of creepy sounds.

But, although it was dark when he reached the shelter, he found the parchment lying there. It must have slipped out while he was asleep.

37

Roaring lions

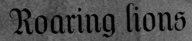

CHRISTIAN PICKED UP THE SCROLL cheerfully. Then he sighed. "I've walked the same road three times! I might have gone *miles* by now!"

Christian continued climbing. And, looking up, he could just see the towers of the Palace Beautiful.

"Perhaps they might put me up for the night," he thought.

So he hurried on. But, as he got nearer, he could hear through the darkness the roaring of lions. Christian nearly ran back, like Scared and Distrust.

But Mr. Watchful, the Palace porter, saw Christian stop, and called, "Don't be scared of the lions! They're on long chains. If you keep to the middle of the path, they won't harm you."

So Christian followed the porter's instructions. But he was shaking with fear. How the lions roared and snapped at him!

A minute later, Christian was through and reached the gate unharmed.

The Palace Beautiful

C AN I STAY HERE TONIGHT?" Christian gasped.

"That depends," said Watchful the porter, looking at him suspiciously. "Who are you? What's your business?"

"My name is Christian. I come from the City of Destruction, and I'm going to the Heavenly City."

"But why are you so late?" asked Watchful. "The sun's already set."

"I would've been here sooner, but I slept in the shelter on the hill," Christian explained. "I dropped my parchment there and had to go back for it."

"Well, that's a sorry tale," said the porter. "I'll call one of the young ladies who live here. If she likes what you say, she might introduce her sisters – otherwise, she might not!"

So Watchful the porter rang the bell, and a beautiful young woman called Mercy appeared. She questioned Christian closely about what had happened on the way. She smiled as he told her, but he saw there were tears in her eyes.

"We have to be very careful who we allow in," she said. "But this house was built for pilgrims. So come in."

He followed her into the house and met her sisters. After supper, they all went to bed. Christian slept in a big bedroom, with windows that opened towards the morning sun.

So, for the moment, he was safe and could rebuild his strength.

41

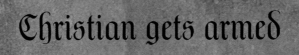
Christian gets armed

EXT MORNING, Christian wanted to continue his journey. But the four sisters – Love, Hope, Mercy and Joy – wouldn't let him leave until they had shown him around. First they took him to the roof.

"If it's clear," they said, "you can see the Mountains of Delight." He saw the beautiful, wooded, sunlit mountains.

"From the top of those mountains you can even see the gates of the Celestial City," said Mercy.

This cheered him up. But that City was still a long way off. Once more Christian wanted to go; but still they kept him.

"Are you married?" asked Love. "Do you have a family?"

"I have a wife and four young children," replied Christian.

"Then why didn't you bring them with you?" she asked.

Christian began to weep. "I would have done," he said. "But they didn't even want *me* to come on this journey. They all stayed behind."

Next the sisters took him to the cellars, where they fitted him with arms to protect him along the way. First, a helmet and breastplate, that could save his life; then a shield, to ward off flaming arrows; then a trusty sword, that could cut through anything; and, finally, shoes that would never wear out.

So, fully armed, Christian hurried at last to the gate.

"Have you seen any other pilgrims pass?" he asked Watchful.

"Yes, one man in recent days."

"Do you know his name?" asked Christian.

"He told me he was Faithful."

"He comes from the town where I was born," Christian exclaimed. "How far ahead do you think he is?"

"By this time, he'll be below the hill," answered the porter.

"Well, porter, goodbye. If I hurry, I may catch him." But he didn't overtake his friend that day.

43

The Valley of Breaking

INSTEAD, Christian found himself in a lonely valley. Here, he stopped to eat the bread and raisins and drink the wine the sisters had given him. He was feeling much happier.

"Perhaps the worst is over," he said to himself.

But, all of a sudden, darkness fell across the sun.

Christian looked up, and saw the Foul Fiend stalking towards him. He was at least nine feet high, and the nearer he came, the more hideous he looked. He had scales like a fish, wings like a dragon, feet like a bear; and out of his mouth belched fire and smoke.

Christian recognized him at once. It was Apollyon!

Terrified, he couldn't decide whether to retreat, or stand and fight. In the nick of time, he remembered he had no protection for his back – so he couldn't run away.

By now the Fiend was very close. "Which stone did you crawl out from?" he roared at Christian.

"I come from the City of Destruction."

"Then you're one of *my* people," said Apollyon. "Because I am the King of that city. Why are you fleeing from me, your King?"

"I may have been born in your land," said Christian. "But now I have *another* king, the King of Kings. I can't turn my back on him."

"You went back on me," replied Apollyon, "yet I'm willing to forget about that."

"The truth is," said Christian, "I'd *rather* serve the King of Kings than serve you."

"But you've already failed him," bellowed Apollyon. "You fell in the Slough of Despond. You slept and dropped your scroll…"

44

"I know. But the King I now serve is merciful and forgiving."

"I'm the enemy of this King," said Apollyon. "I hate him, I hate his laws and I hate his people. Give him the slip, work for me – and I'll double your wages."

"But I know your wages, Apollyon," said Christian. "A person can't *live* on them. They're the wages of death."

45

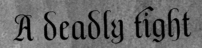
A deadly fight

HEN HE HEARD THIS, Apollyon broke into a rage: "You're right – so now prepare to die!"

"Beware," cried Christian, "I'm on my King's Highway."

But Apollyon barred his path: "I know no fear. I swear you'll go no further!"

He threw a flaming arrow at Christian. But Christian had his shield in his hand, and turned it away. Quickly, he drew his sword, but the Fiend threw arrows as thick as hail. Christian was soon wounded in his head, his hands and feet. He resisted as well as he could, hoping someone might come to his aid. But Christian was growing weaker.

Suddenly Apollyon saw his chance. "Now I have you!" he yelled. He struck Christian so hard that his sword flew out of his hand.

Kneeling on Christian as he lay helpless, Apollyon almost crushed him to death.

But, while Apollyon was preparing his final blow, Christian grabbed his sword, shouting, "When I fall, then I rise." He ran Apollyon through. With a terrible roar the Fiend drew back.

Christian smiled.

Looking up, he saw Apollyon spread his dragon's wings and fly away. The battle was over. But Christian was bleeding. God sent him to the Tree of Life, and he pressed its leaves on all his wounds. He was healed immediately.

Before continuing, Christian sat down to eat. He left his other arms behind, but kept his sword drawn.

"For all I know," he said, "some other enemy is lying in wait for me."

The Valley of the Shadow

HRISTIAN NOW HAD TO ENTER ANOTHER VALLEY – the darkest yet. It was lonely, and there was no water. No one lived there, and it was as silent as the grave.

Suddenly two men ran out from behind some trees, shouting "Back! Go back!"

"Why? What's the matter?" asked Christian.

"Matter! We were going the same way as you're going, and went as far as we dared."

"But what did you meet?" queried Christian.

"Why, the Valley itself," said the men. "It's as black as pitch down there. The only sound is the howling of people who never found their way out. This is the Valley of the Shadow of Death!"

"But this is the only way to the Celestial City," said Christian.

"Well, it's not the way we're going," said the two. And they ran back past him, waving their arms in terror.

But Christian went forward, sword in hand, feeling his way step by step. The path was very narrow; to the right was a deep ditch, into which many had fallen; to the left, a marsh so dangerous that if someone was sucked in, they were never seen again. When Christian tried to avoid the marsh, he nearly fell in the ditch.

48

The air was full of weird voices, and the rush of unseen wings. His sword was no use against them. Sometimes they brushed him and he was afraid they would push him off the path, and he would be lost for ever. For several miles he heard these rushings to and fro, until he could go no further, and wanted to go back.

Then he thought: "By now, I'm probably half-way through. It may be just as dangerous to go back as to go on."

49

Even worse dangers . . .

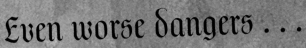

SO CHRISTIAN DECIDED TO GO FORWARD. For a while, silence fell around him again.

Then he thought he heard a man's voice ahead of him, saying: "Although I walk through the Valley of the Shadow of Death, I will fear no evil, for you are with me."

Immediately Christian took courage, because others who loved God were with him in the Valley. He hoped to catch up and join them.

By now, day was dawning, and he could look back. He saw in the distance some of the hobgoblins and dragons that had brushed against him in the dark.

Though the first part of the Valley was very dangerous, the second part was even worse. Christian could see the path ahead was full of pitfalls, traps, and hidden nets. Once he got tangled in a net, and only his sword freed him. Twice a trap snapped shut, almost catching his leg. And time and time again he nearly fell, as the ground crumbled under him.

Then, just when he thought he was out of the Valley, Christian came across a pile of skulls and bones outside a cave – all that remained of pilgrims who had gone that way before.

As he stopped to peer inside the cave, a hand suddenly grasped at him, and tried to grab him by the throat. He leapt back just in time.

Giant Godless lived here, and he had a taste for pilgrims' blood. But he had grown too stiff to walk far. Now all he could do was sit in the cave's entrance, biting his nails in anger because he could no longer harm passing pilgrims.

So Christian hurried safely on his way.

Christian meets Faithful

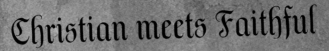

T HEN, CHRISTIAN SAW A MAN RUNNING for his life on the path ahead. It was Faithful, who Watchful had told him about.

"Hi!" he shouted. "Wait till I catch up!"

But Faithful only ran faster, shouting, "There's an enemy at my heels!" (He was still half-crazy with fear, after passing through the Valley.)

Finally, Christian caught up with Faithful. They walked together, telling each other their adventures. The hours passed quickly.

Then Faithful noticed another man on the road ahead.

"Who's that?" he cried, white with fear.

But Christian said, "Why – it's my good friend Evangelist."

And so it was. Evangelist had come to warn them again.

"Don't think you're out of reach of the enemy yet," said Evangelist. "You still have to go through many trials before you enter the Celestial City."

Then he pointed into the distance. "You will soon come to the town of Vanity. You have enemies in that town."

He looked at them sadly.

"Behave like men! For one of you will die painfully there."

Evangelist suddenly vanished again, and Faithful and Christian were left wondering which of them he meant.

53

Vanity Fair

THERE WAS A FAIR ALL THE YEAR ROUND in the town of Vanity. Like other fairs, there were stalls with all sorts of trinkets and knick-knacks for sale – gold and silver, baubles and precious stones.

Cheats, thieves, and pickpockets moved busily among the crowds, and the air was full of swearing and cursing.

Christian and Faithful had to pass through this Fair. Hoping they would go unnoticed, they pulled up their collars around their faces. But the crowd was quick to spot them. First, they made fun of their strange clothes. Then they mocked their foreign accents. Finally, they shouted angrily: "Why aren't you buying our goods? Buy! Buy! Buy!"

"We buy only truth," they said, and stuck their fingers in their ears. But that made the people even angrier, and a riot broke out.

The mayor soon heard the noise. "Arrest those villains, and take away their weapons," he ordered. Officers threw Faithful and Christian into a cage, and stuck their feet in stocks. As they sat there, people came and threw rubbish at them.

Faithful and Christian encouraged each other, saying, "Trust the Lord!" But this enraged the crowds, who started to yell, "Try them! Try them!"

Christian and Faithful are tried

So CHRISTIAN AND FAITHFUL were brought before Judge Hate-good, who called for witnesses.

The first witness, called Envy, pointed a long finger at Faithful. "My lord," he said, "I have known this man for a long time…" (which was a lie). "He is one of the most evil people in this country."

The second witness was Superstition. "This prisoner says that our Religion is nonsense," he declared.

The third witness was Mr. Crawler. "Your Worshipful Lordship Sir," he said, " – and all you very fine gentlemen – I heard this ruffian say things he ought never to have said. He was rude about our noble Prince Beelzebub, and his esteemed friends, Lord De Luxe, Duke Dirty-Mind and Sir Have-it Greedy."

It was clear that Faithful had been picked on by all the witnesses. So the Judge turned on him too.

"You have heard these very fine gentlemen witness against you," he said. "You are obviously a desperate criminal. But I'll hear what you have to say for yourself."

"Your Laws," said Faithful, "are clean against God's Word." At this, the Judge told the jury to reach a verdict.

Mr. Blindman said: "I see clearly this man is crazy."

"Away with him," said Mr No-good.

"Yes," said Mr Nasty, "– I hate the look of him."

"Hang him! Hang him!" said Mr. Headstrong.

"Hanging is too good for him," said Mr Cruelty.

So they found him guilty and killed him.

But I saw in my dream a chariot waiting for Faithful. He was taken up and flew through the clouds, to the sound of trumpets. He arrived first at the Celestial City, and the King gave him a crown of life.

Christian meets Hopeful

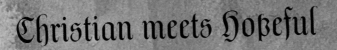

MEANWHILE, WHAT HAD HAPPENED TO CHRISTIAN?

A man called Hopeful was so impressed by Faithful and Christian, that he helped Christian get safely away. So now Christian and Hopeful walked on together.

The road took them near the City of Fine Speech, and four of its most untrustworthy people came out to meet them, bowing low.

"We too are going to the Celestial City," they said. "We should indeed be glad of your company."

Hopeful was all for joining them. But Christian had heard that in their city they worshipped money. He also recognized one of the men as Mr. Facing-both-Ways, a friend of Mr. Money-love.

So Christian whispered in Hopeful's ear, "I don't like the look of them one bit. They're not as nice as they seem."

So, making their excuses, they hurried on.

Doubting Castle

IT WAS JUST AS WELL that Christian had a new friend, Hopeful, for he soon needed his help. They hadn't gone far – the road here was very rough – when they became disheartened. Then Christian noticed a stile that led into a meadow, and looked like a short-cut.

"Here's a better route," he said. "Come on, Hopeful, let's climb over the stile."

"But what if it takes us the wrong way?" asked Hopeful.

"I don't think it will," said Christian. "Look! There's another man walking up ahead."

So over the stile they went, and Christian was glad to find the new path was easier on his feet. But he'd made a terrible mistake. For soon night came, and they completely lost sight of the man ahead.

Then, suddenly, they heard a shriek in the darkness.

"Let's go no further," whispered Hopeful, clutching at Christian's sleeve.

"Who'd have thought this path would lead us nowhere?" Christian exclaimed.

"I was worried about it from the start," admitted Hopeful. "I'd have spoken up earlier, but you're older than me."

"Then let's go back," Christian urged.

But as they tried to turn back, it started to rain. Then lightning flashed and thunder roared.

Soon the rain had washed away the path, and they were in danger of drowning. They found a narrow ledge to shelter on. There they settled, as best they could, and waited for dawn. Worn out, finally they both fell fast asleep.

A dark dungeon

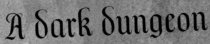

IT WAS BROAD DAYLIGHT when they were woken by a grim voice. "And what d'you think *you're* doing in my grounds?"

Looking up, they saw before them miserable Giant Despair, who owned Doubting Castle.

"We're just poor pilgrims," they said, "and we've lost our way."

"Well, you're trespassing," said the Giant. "And I'm going to teach you a lesson."

The giant threw them into a stinking, dark dungeon. There they lay from Wednesday morning till Saturday night, without a single bite of bread or drop of water.

Giant Despair had a wife. She was even more horrible than him, and he never did anything without asking her advice. So, when the giant went to bed, he told her about the prisoners.

"You're much too soft," she said. "When you get up in the morning, beat them within an inch of their lives!"

So, in the morning, he cut himself a wicked cudgel from a crab-apple tree. Then he beat his prisoners.

Next night, the Giant spoke to his wife again. "What! Are they still alive?" she asked. "When you get up in the morning, tell them to finish themselves off."

A narrow escape

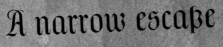

U P GOT THE GIANT, and back he went to the pilgrims.

"Your only way out of here is death," he said. "So why wait? Finish yourselves off!"

He left them rope, a knife, and a bottle of poison, so they could choose how to kill themselves. When they refused, he looked at them in a very ugly way.

He would have killed them himself, except he fell into one of his fits. For the Giant had a secret weakness: in sunny weather, he fell into fits. So he had to go back to bed.

Christian and Hopeful discussed what to do.

"Perhaps the Giant's right," said Christian. "Perhaps death is better than this miserable life."

"But Giant Despair might have another fit," said Hopeful, "and forget to lock us in."

In this way, Hopeful tried to cheer up his friend.

That night, the Giant's wife asked again about the prisoners.

"They refuse to do away with themselves," he told her.

"Then tomorrow morning take them to the castle yard."

Up got the Giant, and took his prisoners to the castle yard.

"These," he said, pointing to the skeletons, "were pilgrims just like you, who trespassed in my grounds. I tore them in pieces, as I will do to you."

A way out

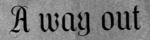

BACK IN THEIR DUNGEON, Christian nearly fainted away. But Hopeful encouraged him. "Brother," he said, "Bear up, and keep on praying."

Then Christian remembered. "In my pocket," he said, "I have an old key called Promise. It just *might* fit the lock."

"Try it," said Hopeful, hopefully.

Mrs Despair was in bed with her husband.

"Perhaps," she said, "they can pick locks – and that's why they haven't given up hope."

"Maybe," said Giant Despair. "I'll search them in the morning."

But even as he was speaking, Christian was trying the dungeon door with his key. The lock was stiff; but at last the key began to turn. After much creaking and groaning, the door swung open, and the light of dawn shone in.

"What's that noise?" said the Giant.

"Better go and see, my dear," said his wife.

Christian and Hopeful ran through the door and then through a great iron gate.

But now the Giant was upon them.

"Nothing can save us!" cried Christian.

But as soon as the Giant came into the sunlight, he had another fit, and his legs gave way. Christian and Hopeful were quickly out of the castle. At the place where they had gone astray, they put up a notice:

THE WAY TO DOUBTING CASTLE.
WARNING: TRESPASSERS
WILL BE DESTROYED.

But they continued safely on the King's Highway.

Mountains of Delight

CHRISTIAN AND HIS NEW FRIEND HOPEFUL now came to the Mountains of Delight, which Christian had seen from the Palace Beautiful. What a refreshing change! After the filth of the Giant's castle, they could wash in a clear stream, and eat fruit from the orchards.

They met shepherds feeding their flocks, who led them to the highest peak.

"If you look through our telescope," said the shepherds, "there's your first glimpse of the Celestial City."

They looked and saw a Golden Gate.

But the shepherds also warned them, "Beware of the Flatterer – and watch out for the Enchanted Ground." And then they sent the pilgrims on their way.

A young fellow called Stupid appeared from a crooked lane ahead of them. He'd set out that very morning from the Country of the Conceited.

"But you didn't come in through the little wooden gate," said Christian, "– you got in by this crooked lane."

"They can't possibly expect me to go all that way back," said Stupid. "I want to get to the Celestial City."

"Then what will you have to show at the Gate of Heaven?" Christian asked. "Have you your scroll?"

"Oh no – I won't need anything like that," said Stupid.

"But they might think you're a robber," warned Christian.

"You do things your way and I'll do them *mine*," said Stupid. "I'm sure all will be well."

So they left him behind.

Another mistake

HRISTIAN AND HOPEFUL soon arrived at a fork in the road, and stood wondering which way to go. A man in white came up, and they thought he was one of the Shining Ones. When they told him they were bound for Heaven's Gate, he said very politely, "I'm going there myself – do follow me."

But the road kept bending round, until the City was right behind them.

"This can't be the right way," said Christian.

Too late! For the next moment they were caught in a net that was stretched across the path. The more they struggled, the more enmeshed they became.

As for the man in white, he threw off his robe. They saw at once that he was a villain. He left them. They might have been there all day, if a true Shining One hadn't appeared, cut the net and set them free.

"Didn't anyone warn you about the Flatterer?" the Angel asked.

"The shepherds did," said Christian. "But we never imagined this nicely-spoken man was the Flatterer."

Soon they were back on the right road again. They saw yet another person coming their way. It was Atheist, and when he heard where they were going, he broke into guffaws of laughter.

"I'm amazed to see how stupid you are," explained Atheist. "Making such a boring journey, and nothing at the end of it."

"Why – don't you think we shall be allowed in?"

"Allowed in?" Atheist repeated. "There's no such place. I've been looking for this city for twenty years. Heaven simply *doesn't* exist."

Then he swept past. But they knew better, having seen the Celestial City through the shepherd's telescope.

Enchanted Ground

AS CHRISTIAN AND HOPEFUL were passing through the next valley, the air became heavy, and they grew very drowsy.

"I can hardly keep my eyes open," yawned Hopeful. "Let's stop, and take a nap. We might wake up refreshed."

"On the other hand," said Christian, "we might never wake. I reckon this is the Enchanted Ground that the Shepherds warned us about."

Hopeful looked aghast at being so foolish.

"If I'd been here on my own," he said, "I would have met my death."

For it felt as if someone had cast a spell on them.

"Let's keep ourselves awake by talking," said Christian.

So, talking without a break, they forced their feet along, and made their escape.

Soon they entered country where the air was sweet. Flowers grew, birds sang, and the sun shone night and day. It was the land of Beulah, where Shining Ones often walked. It was at the frontier of Heaven.

Straight ahead was a perfect view of the Celestial City, higher than the clouds. Its walls and towers shone in the sun, so dazzling that pilgrims could only look at it through dark glass.

75

The Dark River

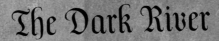

JUST AS THEY THOUGHT THEY WERE SAFE, they stood still, quite stunned. For, between them and the City Gate, flowed a deep, dark river, over which mist swirled. They looked to the left, and looked to the right. But the men on the riverbank said, "You *have* to go through it. There is no bridge."

It was a fearful moment, for Christian couldn't swim. But, after coming all that way, he wouldn't give up now. He stepped trembling into the river, and immediately began to sink.

"Hopeful! Hopeful!" he shouted. "The waves are swallowing me up!"

Hopeful tried to keep Christian's head above water; but the river was so deep that Christian sank again. He was more frightened than he had ever been – even in the Valley of the Shadow.

For this was the River of Death, and he feared he was drowning in it.

Then, all at once, through the mist they saw the sun again. They had new strength, the water was shallower and the ground firmer. And so they reached the shore.

Meanwhile Stupid got across with half their difficulty, and didn't even wet his shoes. He had met a dodgy ferryman called Hopeless, who took him across in his boat.

The Celestial City at last

TWO MEN IN SHINING CLOTHES were standing on the far bank to receive the two friends.

"It's *you* they are waiting for," said Christian to Hopeful. "You've been Hopeful ever since I knew you."

"And so have you," Hopeful replied.

The City stood on a very steep hill, but the pilgrims went up very quickly. Shining Ones took them by the arm. But no one was there to welcome Stupid. He had to climb the path alone.

Then, as the pilgrims neared the Gate, the whole Heavenly City must have known they had arrived. For they were welcomed by the King's Own Trumpeters, who made all Heaven echo with their music.

But when Stupid knocked at the door, the Gate-keeper looked down. "Where's your scroll," he asked, "to prove you came by the right road?"

He fumbled about in his coat, but he had nothing. He stood there silent, then sadly turned back.

But the pilgrims both had their scrolls ready.

A voice called out: "These pilgrims have come from the City of Destruction because they love the King of this Place."

So the Gates of Heaven opened to them, and they entered. And the streets were paved with gold. Good men made perfect walked there. And the bells of the City rang for joy, for Christian and his friend had come to their true home.

After that they shut the gates, and I awoke.

And it was a dream.